ENID BLYTON LIBRARY

Titles in this Series

ISBN 0 86163 096 3

Text copyright 1935 Darrell Waters Limited
Illustrations copyright © 1985 Award Publications Limited

First published as *Nature Tales*
by W. & A.K. Johnston and G.W. Bacon Limited, 1935
This edition first published 1985
Fourth impression 1990

Published by Award Publications Limited, Spring House,
Spring Place, London NW5 3BH, England

Printed in Belgium

Enid Blyton

My Nut I Think!

& Pins and Needles

Illustrated by RENE CLOKE

AWARD PUBLICATIONS

MY NUT I THINK!

The squirrel was collecting nuts for his winter hoard. He had a nice little hiding-place in a hole in his tree.

But the nuthatch
found the hoard.
    The nuthatch was
a fine looking bird with a
very strong beak and he was just as fond
of nuts as the squirrel was.

He didn't sit up
and gnaw a hole in the
shell to get at the kernel,
as the squirrel did.
No, he hadn't teeth like
the squirrel.
He tackled the nut in a
different way.

He took it in his beak and wedged it
tightly in a ridge in the bark of a tree.
  Then, clinging fast to the trunk, he hammered hard at the shell with his strong,
powerful beak.

Crack! He broke the
shell and then ate the nut
inside. Delicious!

Now the squirrel was asleep one day,
when the nuthatch began to hammer at a
nut in the very same tree as the sleeping
squirrel. The squirrel woke up with a
jump and put his head out of the hole to
see what the noise was.

He saw the nut in
the bark of the tree
and felt annoyed. He
ran down to it and
began to try and get
it out with his little
paw.

"My nut, I think!"
he said.

"No, *my* nut!" said the
nuthatch and gave the nut
a peck. It fell to the ground.

The squirrel flew at the
nuthatch, who at once
tried to peck him.

Now, after that, to annoy the squirrel,
the nuthatch always hammered at nuts
just below his sleeping-hole and woke him up.

To make matters worse, he always
chose nuts out of the squirrel's own hoard.

So, time after time, the squirrel would
wake up, leap from his hole and cry, "My
nut, I think!" And then there would be
a squabble and the nut would fall to the
ground.

"I can find the nuts afterwards," thought
the squirrel.

"I will pick up the nuts another time," thought the nuthatch. "What fun it is to annoy this sleepy little squirrel!"

Now, at the bottom of the tree, in a small hole, lived a little mouse. Like the squirrel he hoarded food for the cold days, but he hadn't very much that winter. So when he found nuts falling round him day after day, he was very surprised and pleased.

"There's a lot of hammering and jabbering going on up there!" he thought, looking up into the tree.

"Somebody seems to be throwing away nuts all the time!"

When the squirrel went
down to collect his nuts,
they weren't there!
Not one was to be found.
The nuthatch flew down
too and began to look.

"We'll share them," he said to the
squirrel. "I won't tease you any more."
But there were no nuts to be shared.
"What a peculiar thing!" said the squirrel.
"We'd better go round asking if any one
has seen our nuts!"

There was only
one person who
could tell them
and that was the little mouse
hidden down his hole, with a lovely pile of
nuts. But did he say a word? Not he!

PINS AND NEEDLES

QUICK-FINGERS, the pixie dress-maker, was chased one night by the red goblin.

She ran through
the fields panting
and a small bush
called to her.
    "Quick-Fingers,
hide beneath me!
I will shelter you!"

So Quick-Fingers crawled under the small bush and stayed there safely till the morning. She slept quite soundly, though it rained. But the bush held its leaves over her and not one drop of rain wetted the pixie's frock.

She awoke to hear a munching, crunching sound. "Oh dear, oh dear!" the little bush said. "Here's that great donkey again, eating me as fast as he can. I shall never grow, I shall never grow.

As soon as I clothe
myself with fresh green leaves,
along comes the donkey or the horse or
the sheep; they munch and nibble at me
all day long!"

The pixie was sorry for the little bush.
She took out the needle and spoke to the
donkey. "Donkey, stop eating this bush!
If you don't, I'll prick you!"

The donkey didn't stop, so he got
pricked. He brayed and ran away. The
little bush was surprised that he had gone
so quickly.

"What did you use to prick him
with? What have you got in that box
there?"

"Pins and needles," said Quick-Fingers.
"Oh, little bush, if only you grew pins
and needles round your leaves nobody
would ever come to eat you!"

"Do you know enough magic
to grow me some?"
asked the bush eagerly.

"I think so," said Quick-Fingers. "I'll
set pins and needles all round the edges of
some of your leaves and sing a magic spell
over them. Then they will grow
and all your new leaves will
grow pins and needles
too!"

"Oh, thank you," said the bush, "then
no one will ever want to come and eat me!"

The pixie did as she had said and then
she sang a little spell. She said good-bye
and went. "I'll come back in a month
and see how the magic has worked," she
promised.

When she came back, what a difference
there was in the bush! It had grown well,
for no one had dared to eat it.

Every leaf was set with prickles,
as sharp as needles, as strong as pins!
   "The donkey doesn't come near me!
The horse is afraid of me! The sheep
keep as far away as they can!" said the
bush joyfully. "Now I can grow big.
I can grow into a high tree."

"Well, mind you
don't waste your
pins and needles if you grow tall,"
said the pixie. "No animal can eat
your high-up leaves, so you needn't
bother about pins and needles for them."

Do you know
what the tree is?
Guess! Yes, it's
the prickly holly
tree, and you've
all seen how well
its leaves are set
with pins and needles!

And do you know, the
tree took Quick-Fingers'
advice and didn't grow
prickles on its top
leaves?
That's strange, isn't it?
But if you'll look and
see, you'll find it's true.